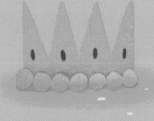

To Eddie, Benji, and Pete, and my amazing mum,
who wisely told me great things take time
— H.R.

To Nana, Grandad, Ma, and Pop x
— S.R.

tiger tales
5 River Road, Suite 128, Wilton, CT 06897
Published in the United States 2022
Originally published in Great Britain 2021
by Little Tiger Press Ltd.
Text copyright © 2021 Holly Ryan
Illustrations copyright © 2021 Siân Roberts
ISBN-13: 978-1-68010-275-8
ISBN-10: 1-68010-275-3
Printed in China
LTP/2800/4078/0821
2 4 6 8 10 9 7 5 3 1

www.tigertalesbooks.com

NEVER MESS WITH A PIRATE PRINCESS!

by

Holly Ryan

Illustrated by

Siân Roberts

tiger tales

Princess Prudence loved her frog,
her bunny, and her spotted dog,
but nothing else could quite compare
to Little Ted, her royal bear.

She took him **here**,
she took him there —

She took that teddy

everywhere . . .

the supermarket

and the zoo . . . .

She took him to the **bathroom**, too!

But once upon a sunny day,
when all the knights went out to play,
the princess took a tiny nap
with Teddy resting on her lap.

It truly was a BIG mistake,
for who should tiptoe past the lake
with skull and crossbones on his chest —
a most unwanted palace guest!

He somersaulted through the air
and **snatched** the royal teddy bear.
Then, leaving Prudence fast asleep,

the pirate fled with one great LEAP!

"Teddy!" Princess Prudence sobbed.
"HELP!" she hollered. "I've been robbed!
Oh, where, oh, where could Teddy be?
I need him back immediately!"

Then all at once, a gallant knight
came charging up in armor bright.
"Fear not, Princess," he boldly said.
"I'm Brave Sir Frank — I'll save your Ted!"

"I don't suppose," asked Princess Prue,
"that I could ride along with you?
I'm more than just a little bored,
and — look! — I even have a sword!"

"You? A knight? Oh, don't be daft!
You're **MUCH** too small!" he rudely laughed.

But Princess Prue was not impressed.

She grabbed some things to help her quest.

Then in a flash, she jumped the moat

and galloped off

She searched the woods
where trees grow tall . . .

a magic glade . . .

a waterfall . . .

a rolling hill . . .

a sandy dune . . . .

She searched
and searched *all*
afternoon.

And could she find that royal bear?
Sadly, no, not **anywhere!**

But wait a minute! Could it be?
A pirate ship upon the sea?
And being poked along the plank
the NOT so bold, or brave, Sir Frank!

The pirates were a frightful sight,
but Prudence was a fearless knight.
"I'll save you, Frank!" the princess cried,
then off she swam against the tide . . .

until with one amazing flip

she leaped on board the pirate ship!

"WHO GOES THERE?"

the pirates roared.

But Prue was quick

and drew her sword.

She tied the pirates to the mast
as Brave Sir Frank just watched aghast.
And there, inside a treasure chest,

she found her bear with royal crest!

Now Princess Prue was firm but fair.
"You pirates can't take teddy bears —
they're very precious friends," she said.
"Stick to things that shine instead!"

"We're sorry!"

cried the naughty brutes.
"They're just so soft and much too cute!
But we'll be good and pack a sack
to take the teddies safely back."

And since good pirates NEVER fib,

that's just exactly what they did.

And now I hear that Princess Prue's
a knight in shining armor, too,
but often likes to take a trip
as captain of the pirate ship.

And while the crew takes care of Frog,
her bunny, and her spotted dog,
she hunts for treasure far and wide
with Teddy safely by her side.

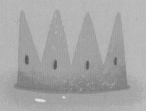